Contents

© Mrs Roger Hargreaves 1991.
Printed and published 1991 under licence from
Price Stern Sloan Inc., Los Angeles.
All rights reserved.
Published in Great Britain by World International
Publishing Limited, an Egmont Company,
Egmont House, PO Box 111, Great Ducie Street,
Manchester M60 3BL.
Printed in Italy.
ISBN 0 7498 0267 7

A lunch to remember

1. Mr Forgetful was a little forgetful. You can say that again. Mr Forgetful was a little forgetful. One morning in Forget-me-not Cottage, which was where he lived, the telephone rang. It was Mr Happy.

2. "Just thought I'd remind you. We're meeting for lunch today. One o'clock at Lucky's," he said. Mr Forgetful was silent. "You've forgotten, haven't you?" laughed Mr Happy. Mr Forgetful thought. "Forgotten what?" he said.

3. Mr Forgetful set off for town. "Lucky's at one. Lucky's at one," he said over and over to himself. On the way he met Mr Nosey. "Where are you off to?" Mr Nosey asked. "The Sticky Bun," replied Mr Forgetful.

4. When he reached town, Mr Forgetful went to the restaurant. The wrong one! By the time he remembered which was the right one, he was nearly an hour late. Mr Happy was waiting outside. "I'm glad you didn't forget," he smiled.

5. The two friends were shown to a table, and looked at the menu. The waitress came up to take their orders. "What will you have to start?" she asked. Mr Forgetful looked puzzled. "Start what?" he said.

6. They both decided on soup, but when the waitress brought it, Mr Forgetful couldn't remember whether he'd asked for chicken or oxtail. But they sorted that out, and enjoyed the rest of the meal, and soon it was time to go.

7. Mr Forgetful spent a long time trying to remember where he had put his hat. And some more time trying to remember which hat was his. But finally he found the right one, and he and Mr Happy said goodbye, and left.

8. "I think I'd better see you home," laughed Mr Happy. "You've probably forgotten the way!" As they walked along, chatting happily, a small figure in the distance called, "Sir, sir. You've forgotten to pay the bill."

Little Miss Dotty's SOCCER SPECIAL

It was the end of August. Clear blue sky. Hot sunshine. Holidays.
Little Miss Dotty was on her way to buy an ice-lolly when she met
Mr Rush. "Are you coming to the football match?" he called. "It's the
start of the new season." Little Miss Dotty did not have time to reply
because Mr Rush had rushed off. "I *would* like to go!" she said.

Little Miss Dotty hurried home. She had been to a football match
last Christmas and got very cold standing on the touchline. So she put on
a coat. A warm one. With a fleecy lining. Then she put on another coat.
An even warmer one. With a thermal lining, fur collar and fur cuffs. And
she ran all the way to the park. How dotty can you get?

The match had just started when Little Miss Dotty arrived. "Good
game, isn't it!" yelled Mr Noisy, twirling his football rattle. "Splendid!"
agreed Little Miss Splendid. "I'm not enjoying it," gasped Little Miss
Dotty. "I'm so HOT!"

Meanwhile, on the pitch, Mr Strong had the ball. Nobody dared to tackle him because he was so strong. Mr Strong dribbled the ball up the field and booted it at the goal. It went like a rocket. No, that's not true! It went like a jet-powered, supersonic space rocket! CRACK! The ball hit the crossbar and the whole goal shattered into a hundred pieces. Maybe a thousand. Possibly a million. "Oh dear!" thought Little Miss Dotty.

The game continued. But the missing goalposts caused lots of trouble. "I scored just then!" claimed Mr Grumpy. "No you didn't!" argued Mr Uppity. "You missed by a mile." "I said I scored!" yelled Mr Grumpy.

"Didn't!" retorted Mr Uppity.

"Did!"

"Didn't!"

And so on. And on. And on.

"Oh dear!" thought Little Miss Dotty again.

Then Little Miss Dotty had an idea. It just popped into her brain. Usually, ideas pop into Little Miss Dotty's brain and pop out again. But this one stayed there. Because it was a good one!

Little Miss Dotty took off her coat with the thermal lining, fur collar and cuffs. Next she took off her coat with the fleecy lining. Holding one on one arm and one on the other, Little Miss Dotty marched onto the pitch and plonked the coats down on the ground. "You can use *these* as goalposts," she said.

How everyone cheered! First of all they cheered when Mr Grumpy scored a goal and nobody argued about it. Then they cheered Little Miss Dotty for having such a clever idea and saving the match. "It's my pleasure," she giggled. "I feel cool for the first time today."

Her face was still red, though.

With embarrassment.

A BAD DREAM

1. One evening, Mr Lazy was in bed reading his favourite bedtime book called *Sleepytime Tales*.

2. But Mr Lazy was so lazy that he read only one page, then he yawned and fell sound asleep.

3. Suddenly, there came a loud knock at the door. Mr Lazy got up and went downstairs to open it.

4. It was Little Miss Bossy. "WAKE UP, WAKE UP!" she said. "There's lots of WORK to be done!"

5. Mr Lazy groaned as Little Miss Bossy marched him into the kitchen. "First, the WASHING UP!" she said.

6. After that, she ordered Mr Lazy to wash his socks, dust all the furniture and polish the floor.

7. And so it went on . . . until the next morning, when Mr Lazy woke up! It had all been a terrible dream.

8. "Phew!" sighed Mr Lazy. "That dream *was* hard work!" Then do you know what? He went back to sleep!

The Mr Men and Li

Mr Clever and Little Miss Star have set some questions to find out how much you know about their famous friends. Mr Topsy-Turvy has the answers at the bottom of the page.

5 Which LITTLE MISS once visited Miseryland and cheered up the King with her happy smile?
a) LITTLE MISS HELPFUL
b) LITTLE MISS SUNSHINE
c) LITTLE MISS DOTTY

6 Which MR MAN can do things that aren't normally possible – like becoming invisible?

1 What is MR STRONG's favourite food?
a) eggs
b) cheese
c) curry

2 What sort of shoes stop LITTLE MISS BOSSY being bossy?
a) high heels
b) riding boots
c) bossyboots

3 MR SKINNY lives in Fatland.
a) True?
b) False?

4 Can you fill in the missing name?
MR _ _ _ _ _ _ lives in a house underneath a daisy at the bottom of Mr Robinson's garden.

MASTERMIND QUIZ

7 Which of the MR MEN snores "like a herd of elephants"?
a) MR SMALL
b) MR QUIET
c) MR NOISY
d) MR LAZY

8 LITTLE MISS NAUGHTY wears a big, red bow on the top of her head.
a) True?
b) False?

9 What is the name of LITTLE MISS NEAT's cottage?
a) Spickandspan Mansion
b) Twopin Cottage
c) Trim Towers

10 Who lives next door to MR SLOW?
a) MR SNOW
b) MR DIZZY
c) MR BOUNCE
d) MR BUSY
e) MR TICKLE

1. a) eggs 2. c) bossyboots 3. a) true 4. SMALL 5. b) LITTLE MISS SUNSHINE 6. MR IMPOSSIBLE 7. c) MR NOISY 8. b) false. It is a big, GREEN bow 9. b) Twopin Cottage 10. d) MR BUSY

Mr Strong's Egg-stravaganza

Mr Strong wants you to help him sort these eggs. Can you count how many brown eggs, white eggs and speckled eggs there are? Write your answers on the hen baskets at the bottom of the page.

BROWN   WHITE   SPECKLED

16

Mr Slow's Stopping Train

Help Mr Slow find his way to the station.

Little Miss Scatterbrain Saves The Day

1. One morning, Little Miss Scatterbrain woke up to find it had been snowing. Hard! "I must go shopping," she said. "My larder's empty!"

2. Little Miss Scatterbrain searched for her purse. "I had it yesterday," she muttered. Can YOU see where it is? Of course. In her hand! What a scatterbrain!

3. Little Miss Scatterbrain set off for the shops. "I've left my shopping list behind," she cried. "I'll have to remember what I want – a loaf of bread, a packet of salt and a carton of milk."

4. "A loaf of bread, a packet of salt and a carton of milk," recited Little Miss Scatterbrain. She reached the grocer's shop. "A carton of bread, a loaf of salt and a packet of milk, please," she said.

5. It took the grocer half an hour to sort out the order. "What a scatterbrain!" he sighed. Little Miss Scatterbrain left the shop – leaving her shopping bag behind!

6. On the way home, Little Miss Scatterbrain took a short cut through the park. (Except that it was the long way round!) She saw some hungry birds and an even hungrier cat. And she saw Mr Bump slip over. For the tenth time. "Horrid snow!" she said.

7. Little Miss Scatterbrain sat down on a park bench to rest. When she got up, she left her loaf of bread behind her. The hungry birds swooped down and pecked at it.

8. Then Little Miss Scatterbrain felt thirsty. "I'll open this carton of milk," she said. Of course, she opened the packet of salt instead! And she spilt it on the path.

9. The salt melted the ice on the path. "HURRAY!" cheered Mr Bump. "Now I can walk without slipping over." And he did – until he bumped into a tree!

10. Little Miss Scatterbrain reached the park gates. She dropped the carton of milk. It spilt on the ground. "How very kind!" thought the even hungrier cat.

11. Little Miss Scatterbrain reached home at last. She went to put her shopping away. "It's GONE!" she gasped. No bread. No salt. No milk!

12. There was a knock on the door. It was the mayor. "Congratulations!" he boomed. "You've won our Helpful Citizen Award!"

"What for?" exclaimed Little Miss Scatterbrain.

13. The mayor explained how Little Miss Scatterbrain had helped the birds, the cat and Mr Bump. "You won't need any food," he said. "I'm inviting you to a banquet."

Little Miss Scatterbrain was guest of honour at the banquet. "I'm glad I'm scatterbrained, after all," she giggled.

MR SMALL'S NIGHT OUT

This story is all about Mr Small, who is probably the smallest person in the world. He lives in a tiny house at the bottom of Mr Robinson's garden. Underneath a daisy. That's how small he is!

One Christmas Eve, Mr Small had gone into town and had spent the day enjoying himself.

He had bought a Christmas present for Mr Robinson in the morning.

Then he treated himself to an excellent lunch at his favourite restaurant. He had ordered a three-course lunch.

Two chips and a pea!

Which was quite a lunch for somebody as small as Mr Small.

In the afternoon, Mr Small had visited the library to change his library book.

Unfortunately, the book he wanted was on the top shelf. It took Mr Small all afternoon to climb up the steps to get it because he had to keep stopping for a rest.

And it was nearly closing down time by the time he had climbed down again.

So you see how difficult some things were for Mr Small.

Then Mr Small had to run all the way to the bus stop to catch the last bus home. But the bus driver didn't see him and drove off without him.

Poor Mr Small!

He began to walk along the road. It was getting dark and it was beginning to snow.

Big, thick snowflakes fell from the sky.

Now, if you're as small as Mr Small, one snowflake is like a great snowball landing on your head.

Thud!

So, you can imagine what it was like for Mr Small to be caught in a snowstorm, can't you?

Thud! Thud! Thud!

Mr Small did look miserable. It was getting late and Mr Small thought it would probably take him all night to walk home.

If not all the next day.

And the next.

He was beginning to wonder if he would ever get home, when suddenly he heard the sound of sleigh bells.

Mr Small looked up and there, flying towards him was, guess who?

Father Christmas!

"Hello," said Father Christmas, bending down and picking Mr Small up out of the snow. "You shouldn't be out on a night like this!"

"Hello," said a very surprised Mr Small. "How did you know I was here?"

Father Christmas winked.

"I know everything," he smiled. "Or rather," he added, looking worried, "everything, that is, *except* how to deliver this little parcel."

"I am much too big to get into a mousehole," said Father Christmas sadly.

"But I'm not!" laughed Mr Small. "If you take me there, I'll deliver this parcel for you. Little Miss Tiny is a special little friend of mine."

So Father Christmas put Mr Small inside his fur pocket, which was a very warm and snug place to be, and flew off to Home Farm.

Mr Small crept into Little Miss Tiny's mousehole and put the tiny parcel into her stocking. The he crept out again.

The smallest Father Christmas in the world!

Father Christmas handed Mr Small a tiny parcel. It was addressed to:

Little Miss Tiny
The Mousehole
Home Farm

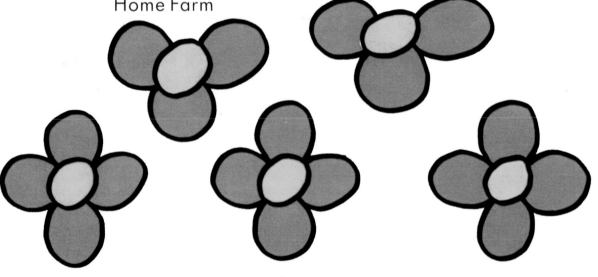

"Now it's home for you," said Father Christmas.

And he took Mr Small safely back to his tiny house, underneath a daisy, at the bottom of Mr Robinson's garden.

"I've got just one more present to deliver," smiled Father Christmas, reaching into his sack.

"Who for?" asked Mr Small.

"You!" laughed Father Christmas, and handed Mr Small a parcel.

"But you mustn't open it until tomorrow morning," he said. "Goodbye now, and Happy Christmas!"

Mr Small was so excited, he hardly slept a wink that night.

Early the next morning, he sat up in bed and opened his present.

It was the perfect gift.

Something he had always wanted.

A special, fully automatic, thermostatically controlled, electric toaster.

Can you guess what was so special about it?

I'll tell you.

It toasted . . . one crumb at a time!

Mr Men Party Masks

Trace the Mr Men onto some thick white drawing paper, and colour them with your felt tips or crayons.

string

eye hole

eye hole

string

Mr Bump

Mr Strong

Then cut them out round the outline, cut out the eye holes, and tie strings long enough to go round your head, at the sides, in the positions shown.

29

Mr Busy's Parcel Problem

Can you rearrange the letters to help Mr Busy deliver these parcels? The labels are all Mr Men names. Write your answers in the boxes below.

3. MR. C ONÜBE

1. MR. G TSRNO

4. MR. G OWRN

5. MR. S INKYN

6. MR. ES ENEZS

2. MR. C M ESFIHI

1	
2	
3	

4	
5	
6	

Little Miss Scatterbrain's Shopping List

Crack the code to discover what Little Miss Scatterbrain wants to buy from the butcher!

THE CODE

A	B	C	D	E	F	G	H	I	J	K	L	M	N	O	P	Q	R	S	T	U	V	W	X	Y	Z
B	D	F	H	J	L	N	P	R	T	V	X	Z	Y	W	U	S	Q	O	M	K	I	G	E	C	A

THE CLUE

B
X B Q N J
X W B L
W L
D Q J B H

THE ANSWER

At the bus stop

A story without words

34

What a sneeze! Little Miss Scatterbrain's hat ha[s]
landed on top of Mr Funny's head. But where h[as]
his gone? Who is wearing Little Miss Bossy's h[at]?
And what has happened to Mr Small's?

Little Miss Shy's
Marvellous Marbles

Little Miss Shy always played on her own. If anyone asked her to join in a game, she would always reply: "No, thank you. I'm too shy." Shy by name and shy by nature.

If it was raining, Little Miss Shy played cards. Patience and Solitaire were her favourite games. If it was sunny, she went outside and did some skipping. Today, however, Little Miss Shy had decided to play marbles.

On her own.

Outside her house.

Little Miss Shy was enjoying her game when along came Mr Clever. "I'd hurry up and finish your game if I were you," he warned. "There's a storm coming. I heard it on the weather forecast."

With that, he went on his way without treading on a single crack in the pavement all the way home. Isn't that clever?

"I'll just have one last shot," thought Little Miss Shy.

FLICK! Little Miss Shy rolled her final marble into the circle chalked on the pavement. Suddenly, round the corner, came Mr Busy. "Must get my shopping before the storm breaks!" he cried. "And I want to wash the car, clean the windows and dig the garden!" What a busy fellow!

Mr Busy did not see Little Miss Shy's marbles on the pavement in front of him. WHOOPS! He slipped on them, hitting the ground with a bump that even Mr Bump would have been proud of!

Little Miss Shy helped Mr Busy to his feet. "I'm not hurt," he cried, dusting himself down. "Must get on. Bye!" And Mr Busy hurried off, not caring how many cracks in the pavement he trod on.

Little Miss Shy looked round for her marbles. She saw them rolling down a drain. PLOP! PLOP! PLOP! "They're lost!" she wailed.

Little Miss Shy had no time to feel sad.

BOOM! FLASH! The storm had arrived!

Little Miss Shy hurried indoors and hid under the bedclothes. She did not like thunderstorms. Do you? Bit frightening, aren't they? Anyway, instead of the usual HISS of pouring rain, Little Miss Shy heard a loud drumming noise on the roof of her house. It sounded like Mr Noisy playing a hundred drums — and you can imagine how noisy that would be! Little Miss Shy peeped out to see what was going on.

It was hailing! Not little tiny hailstones like peas. No. Great big, whopping hailstones like ping-pong balls. Like gobstoppers. Like MARBLES.

When the storm passed, Little Miss Shy ventured outside to look at the giant hailstones. She picked one up and rolled one along the ground. It ran as smooth as ice. Because it *was* ice! "I'll play with these instead!" she giggled.

Little Miss Shy started her game again. With the giant hailstone marbles.

Mr Sneeze and Mr Snow saw what she was doing and asked if they could join in the game.

"Sorry," said Little Miss Shy. "I'm too shy."

Then she thought for a moment.

And she thought for another moment.

"Maybe I'm not," she whispered.

Mr Funny Wins a Cup

1. Mr Funny was having lunch. Fish finger soup! He was enjoying a second cup of soup when there was a knock at the door of his funny teapot house. He went to see who it was.

2. There, on the doorstep, was Little Miss Dotty. "Hello," said Mr Funny. "You look lost." Miss Dotty sighed. "I am," she said. "I can't find my way home to Nonsenseland, and I want to be back for the Nonsense Cup competition."

3. As you may know, every year in Nonsenseland the King awards a Cup to the person with the silliest idea of the year. "Don't worry," smiled Mr Funny, "I'll take you home in my car." Mr Funny's car is a shoe!

4. As Mr Funny and Miss Dotty drove along in Mr Funny's shoe, everybody laughed at such a funny sight. Even the flowers giggled to themselves. Then Mr Funny noticed the grass was blue. They were in Nonsenseland.

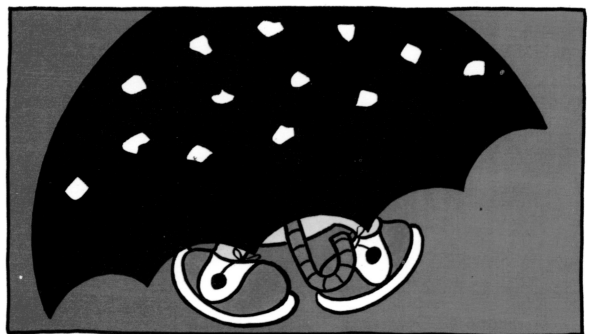

5. Mr Funny drove into the City Square just as Mr Nonsense was showing his silly idea to the crowd. It was an umbrella. Full of holes. "To water the plants when it rains," he explained. The crowd clapped.

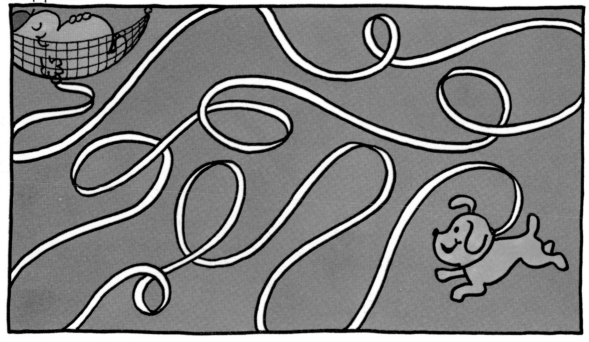

6. Then it was Mr Silly's turn. He had invented an elasticated dog lead for lazy people who didn't like walking the dog! Isn't that silly? The crowd cheered, and Mr Silly felt sure he would win the Cup.

7. The King stood up. "Ladies and gentlemen," he said to the crowd. "We have seen some very silly ideas today, and so it is my pleasure to . . ." And then he stopped. He was looking at Mr Funny's car in amazement.

8. "Whose car is that?" cried the King. "Why, it's a shoe. How silly!" Little Miss Dotty called out, "It's Mr Funny's car," and Mr Funny blushed. "That," said the King, "is quite the silliest idea ever! Mr Funny has won the Cup!"

Mr Greedy's Fruity Crossword

apple
banana
grape
lemon
peach

pear
plum
raspberry
strawberry

Mr Greedy is off to market to buy some fruit for his mid-morning snack! He has listed the fruits he wants – but he has left out one of his favourites. Can you fit the names of the fruits into the crossword, using the coloured letters that are already there to help you?

Now write the coloured letters on the line below:

— — — — — — — —

Unscramble these letters to discover the name of the fruit Mr Greedy has forgotten:

Little Miss Twins

Here's a double delight – two delicious recipes served up by the Little Miss Twins. To make them you will need some help from a grown-up, and the use of the oven. So don't ignore Mr Clever's warning.

ALWAYS HAVE AN ADULT PRESENT WHEN YOU USE THE KITCHEN!

CHOCOLATE FLAPJACKS

<u>What you need:</u>
300g porridge oats
3 tablespoons golden syrup
150g margarine
75g sugar
some dark cooking chocolate

<u>What you do:</u>
Preheat the oven to gas mark 3/160° C/325°F.
1. Melt the golden syrup, margarine and sugar in a large saucepan.
2. Remove from the heat and stir in the porridge oats.
3. Transfer the mixture to a greased baking tin, pressing it down flat.
4. Place in the centre of the oven and bake for about 20-30 minutes until golden brown. Leave to cool.
5. Melt the chocolate in another saucepan and spread over the flapjacks.
6. Leave to cool again. Then cut into squares.

Twin Recipe Page

CINNAMON COCONUT COOKIES

What you need:

100g margarine
50g sugar
75g plain flour
50g semolina
25g desiccated coconut
1 level teaspoon cinnamon

What you do:

Preheat the oven to gas mark 3/160° C/325°F.

1. Using a wooden spoon, cream the margarine and sugar together until the mixture is light and fluffy.

2. Add the coconut and cinnamon and mix well. Add the flour and semolina and mix well.

3. Press the mixture together several times with your hands. Form into balls using a teaspoon.

4. Place balls well apart on greased baking tray, flatten slightly and bake until firm and golden brown. Leave for a minute to cool. Transfer to a wire rack.

Mr Greedy's Menu Mates

What will Mr Greedy choose for his meal? Everything! Look at the plates on the table and pair the food into five familiar things to eat. Then write your answers on the menu.

MENU

B and D
A and H
I and F
G and C
E and J

Mr Worry's Weather Wordsearch

Poor Mr Worry. He does worry. About the weather especially! Hidden in this puzzle are twenty words about the weather. See if you can find them all. They read across, or down, or diagonally.

BREEZE
CLOUD
DRIZZLE
FLOOD
FOG
FROST
GALE
HAIL
HEATWAVE
ICE
LIGHTNING
MIST
RAIN
SHOWER
SLEET
SNOW
STORM
SUNSHINE
THUNDER
WIND

```
          S N O W
          X U M I S T A
      F O G G N D F C L O U D
    F L G R U S V R L R I E T
    M O S I E H F O I O C C H
    O P R A I N S G Z E Z U
    D N G U N R T H S Z S N U
  U B B R E E Z E T T M L D N
  H E A T W A V E N O J E E A
  C L O O M D J G I R K E R V
  A H H A I L Q E N M M T T I
  S V W I N D W G A L E Y
```

Little Miss Splendid's Picnic Surprise

1. It was a sunny day and Little Miss Splendid was tired of being in the house. "I think I'll go for a splendid picnic," she announced. Little Miss Splendid packed her picnic basket, picked up her folding chair, and set off for the countryside.

2. She found a splendid spot. Under a tree. Beside a stream. "I'll set out my picnic," she thought, spreading out her picnic cloth.

3. There were sandwiches, a cream cake and some biscuits. It looked so splendid that Little Miss Splendid closed her eyes in admiration. "Everything I do," she sighed, "is so . . . so . . . SPLENDID!"

4. Some squirrels from the tree above thought the picnic looked splendid, too. They ran off with the sandwiches! ''Come back, you scoundrels!'' yelled Little Miss Splendid.

5. The squirrels took no notice. They gobbled up the sandwiches. Then Mr Silly approached. He was out jogging. But, being Mr Silly, he was jogging BACKWARDS! Isn't that silly?

6. Of course, Mr Silly could not see where he was going. He ran through the middle of Little Miss Splendid's picnic and trod on the cream cake. SQUELCH! A jet of cream squirted into Little Miss Splendid's face!

7. ''You SILLY man!'' scolded Little Miss Splendid, wiping the cream from her face. ''Thank you,'' said Mr Silly. ''YOO-HOO!'' called a familiar voice.

8. It was Mr Tickle. "May I join you?" he asked politely. Little Miss Splendid liked anyone polite. "Of course," she replied. So Mr Tickle helped himself to the biscuits. With his long arms. Across the stream!

9. Mr Tickle ate the biscuits, raised his hat again politely, and departed. Now Little Miss Splendid had *nothing* left of her picnic. "I'll just sit here and look splendid!" she decided.

10. Suddenly there was a loud roar. ROAR! A cloud of dust covered Little Miss Splendid. "UGH!" she spluttered. "COUGH! COUGH!"

11. The dust was coming from Mr Funny and Mr Noisy. They were having a car race. "They don't know who's the winner," complained Little Miss Tiny, "so they won't stop."

12. Suddenly, Little Miss Splendid had an idea. A splendid idea! She tied her picnic cloth to a stick and waved it at the racing cars as they sped past. The black and white squares looked just like a proper motor-racing flag! Mr Funny and Mr Noisy screeched to a halt. "It's a dead heat!" announced Little Miss Splendid. "You're *both* winners!" Everyone was so pleased that the noisy, dirty race was over that they treated Little Miss Splendid to a slap-up meal in a restaurant. "This is simply splendid!" she beamed.

Mr Mischief's New Year

One New Year's Eve, Mr Mischief was sitting at home making a list of New Year's resolutions. Not good ones. Oh no! Not Mr Mischief. He was making a list of all the naughty things he was going to do in the New Year.

He was still writing when his clock struck midnight. And that gave Mr Mischief the idea for his naughtiest trick yet.

Mr Mischief got up, went to a cupboard and found a small box.

Then he took the box and ran out of the house as fast as his little legs would carry him.

He ran all the way into town, giggling as he ran. He couldn't wait to try out his latest piece of mischief.

When Mr Mischief reached the town, he went straight to the Town Hall and looked up at the clock. Then, when he was quite sure no one was looking, he went to a little door at the side of the Town Hall and opened it.

Inside was a staircase that led all the way up to the Town Hall clock. Mr Mischief ran up the stairs faster than his little legs could carry him. Which is very fast, I can tell you.

At the top of the stairs, Mr Mischief stopped and listened.

Tick, tock. Tick, tock.

The Town Hall clock was ticking away as it had always done. Day in. Day out. It was the best clock for miles around and everyone depended on it.

Mr Mischief listened again.

Tick, tock. Tick, tock.

Then, he crept right up to the clock, and opened the box. Can you guess what he was going to put inside?

Tick, tock. Tick, tock.

Mr Mischief reached out and took the tick, tock right out of the clock and popped it into his box.

And, of course, you know what happened to the clock, don't you? It stopped. Not a tick or a tock to be heard.

"Got you!" giggled Mr Mischief as he ran down the stairs. "Ooo, what glorious mischief," he chuckled as he skipped outside. "First trick of the year!"

Just at that moment, Mr Happy came round the corner. He was on his way home from a party.

"Happy New Year!" said Mr Happy. "What have you got in that box?"

Mr Mischief tried to hide it behind his back. "Er . . . it's just a little New Year's Eve surprise," he said and ran off home.

"Hm?" thought Mr Happy. "I wonder what Mr Mischief has been up to?"

The next morning, there was chaos!

Everyone was late because the clock had stopped.

The milkman was late delivering Mr Happy's milk.

The news reader on the radio was late reading the news. He read the seven o'clock news at half-past ten!

The policeman on traffic duty was late. The town was full of angry drivers all stuck in traffic jams.

And Mr Greedy's favourite restaurant was late opening. The waiter served breakfast when he should have been serving lunch and lunch when he should have been serving tea!

Everyone was very cross.

Mr Clever went along to the Town Hall to have a look at the clock, to see if he could mend it. After all, Mr Clever is the cleverest person in the world.

"What is the matter with it?" asked Mr Happy.

"Er . . ." began Mr Clever. "I'm afraid I don't know."

"Well, that's not very clever of you, is it?" said Mr Happy. Then he thought for a moment and said, "But there is someone who might know. Someone I remember who was here last night with a little New Year's Eve surprise in a box . . ."

Later that day, Mr Happy went to call on Mr Mischief. He took a friend with him. Little Miss Magic!

Mr Mischief opened the door. "Hello," he said. "What do you want?"

"Nothing much," smiled Mr Happy. "Just a little of your . . . time."

"It won't take more than a tick," smiled Little Miss Magic, quickly stepping inside and spotting the box.

"A tick and a tock at the very most," grinned Mr Happy, winking at Little Miss Magic.

Then Little Miss Magic pointed to the box and said, "OPEN!"

And it did!

Then Little Miss Magic told the tick, tock to start ticking.

And it did!

Tick, tock. Tick, tock.

"LOUDER!" ordered Little Miss Magic.

And it did! Tick, tock! TICK, TOCK! Louder and louder until Mr Mischief begged it to stop.

"Promise there will be no more naughty tricks!" said Little Miss Magic, sternly.

"What! No more tricks?" cried Mr Mischief.

"Promise, or else," said Little Miss Magic drumming her fingers on the box.

"Oh, all right," said Mr Mischief.

Then Little Miss Magic commanded the ticking to stop and closed the box.

"Time to go," said Mr Happy.

"We must put the tick, tock back into the Town Hall clock."

"No sooner said than DONE!" smiled Little Miss Magic and she opened the box to let the tick, tock fly back to the Town Hall.

"That's amazing!" laughed Mr Happy.

"I know," smiled Little Miss Magic. "I suppose you could say, it's amazing how . . . time flies!"

61